MYSTERIES OF LIFE

By
Tony Gomes

*We at Trafford believe that it is the responsibility of us all, as both individuals
and corporations, to make choices that are environmentally and socially sound.
You, in turn, are supporting this responsible conduct each time you purchase a
Trafford book, or make use of our publishing services. To find out how you are
helping, please visit www.trafford.com/responsiblepublishing.html*

*Our mission is to efficiently provide the world's finest, most comprehensive
book publishing service, enabling every author to experience success.
To find out how to publish your book, your way, and have it available
worldwide, visit us online at www.trafford.com*

Revision date: 10/14/2009

 www.trafford.com

North America & international
toll-free: 1 888 232 4444 (USA & Canada)
phone: 250 383 6864 ♦ fax: 812 355 4082

Table of Contents

In Search of God

———•◆•———

Despite discarding their belief in a personal God, some people believe in a creator, because they are convinced that the designs evident in nature require an intelligent designer. Although science is a "mightier" tool that keeps digging up new secrets about the universe and the life on our planet, scientists still face many fundamental questions that never seem to end and may not ever be answered.

Questions about the origin of the universe, about life here on Earth, or about what existed before the origin of the universe can deeply dampen one's beliefs, including those of major scientists.

Many other discoveries, failures, studies, and controversial theories, regardless of their objective to prove or disprove the existence of God, might help us enchant our personal beliefs, religiously or non-religiously. Sometimes God is referred to as an intelligent being or "thing" that somehow regulated all the cosmic laws rather than as a savior or personal God, as taught in diverse religions.

When the Big Bang theory fails in part to explain the universe and its birth, it makes you question.

When the four fundamental physical forces, (strong and weak nuclear force, Gravity, and electromagnetism) are in a most precise degree thereafter, make possible the existence of the universe and of life makes you wonder.

Our DNA suggests that maybe things are not just a big coincidence; that there is an intelligent designer behind all this, and maybe the universe did not happen by chance. Nevertheless, the majority of scientists completely discard the idea of a personal God. Many more of the universe's complex designs remain a puzzle to scientific implications, but whether or not you believe in God is a personal "choice."

The question at hand is how or in what way science might help us find God, thanks to the hard work of scientists who constantly reveal the mysteries of the universe and life, therefore leading some to realize that there's the possibility of an intelligent designer, due to the complexity and "perfection" exuded by our surroundings. Skeptics exist on both sides, and in the end, the ultimate choice will be yours, for it is not just a matter of debate or trivia, but also a question that will have a big impact in your future.

There is much more to it, from life experience and questions that you yourself have not gotten the chance to unravel. I personally do not believe scientists can prove the existence of God unless they have the power of contradicting God's invisibility (some believe only what they see) and many other reasons, but it might influence your belief in determining whether there is or not there is a God.

Reflections—Human Understandings

Humans have many facets and multidimensional understandings, one of which consists of spirituality and "fiction." Therefore, when we dwell on it, we imagine gazillions of possibilities of an ideal life and can theorize on them individually. The fruition to adapt is compulsive and can be rewarding as an enrichment of life, and then depart in a more complex level that is more spiritual than physical, then reciprocated ourselves into this environmental pastry when we find ourselves "kryptonite".

Reality exists in conjunction with our subconscious, manifesting our "dance," passions, sounds, gestures, intuitions, and reflections-in-meditation. We express ourselves and enchant our problems with no postdate whatsoever. However, the dimension of anything will be the ultimate. The more we can be, or "accomplish," especially when there is not a measurement for existence itself, is in comparison to achievements. Whatever is the result, the satisfaction is relative for each one of us, and only then can we generate future descendants to carry on.

Question: Will we know the ultimate?

Yes, but are words really a tool of revelation? "Actions speak louder than words."

Maybe we will find an answer by doing more than talk about it. However, it can be reciprocated back and forth, again enabling us to focus on the parallels of life. It seems indifferent, but is very common—this not to elude nor conspire our abilities, but it is simply the way it is...

The acceptance of weakness is a virtue, known limitation and experimentation is not just for the thrilled of it, but to survive and understand throughout wisdom. It is perhaps the bigger steps in all existence: knowing where we are, where we stand, and the ability to make our own destiny to fulfill when the time's due, taking further steps as we head into the future. Growing shall be necessary, not for us, for time's running short, but for the generation yet to come. They will need to act quicker, faster, stronger, and "better" than we in current events do.

We will be much stronger and smarter. There will be not mere futile desires to fulfill with short pleasures, but we will be able to adapt to create and install a society that we now cannot even begin to imagine. Nevertheless, know it is possible, it is achievable, and it is the beauty of life—the ultimate "The." No one is deprived, and everyone is thriving— human race together, hand-in-hand in the cosmos, not individually, with self-praise decoded in our metabolism.

The acquaintance sustained in the migratory ecosystem redeems upon individuals characters put into perspective in a non-judgmental aspect of the bios, sided in equivalence.

Sure there is an abomination that lays under every inch of the substance. The prerogative carries within elements sub-consequently divided from a premature nature that yields "success" in possession of micro-cosmos (universe) reachable for all of us. Beneficial greatness is rewarded to single-individuals, because he shows and expresses the little power he has. Now imagine the entire race in one. It would be much more powerful so why not use it then. We have tried everything, so let it be known that the journey continues.

Inner Struggles

Slaves to our desires, we surrender.
Human race, thin willpower gives in.
Thrilled, we headed for destruction,
Expressing our struggles, everything seems in vain.
Or can we catch the wind?

Shortness pleasures, with everlasting put into us,
Making us look timeless within the Cosmos.
Our destination is to rejoice in such desperation,
Not knowing if it is an outburst or euphoria.
We named it mysteries.

Doomed when released to this world, it is a loot.
Suppress to what future holds in, we wait.
The key is to keep it anonymous,
But reality makes us hesitate and anticipate,
Therefore, we don't know where we are.
Perhaps, can we change our destiny?

Thinking in miniature, wishing a better life,
We fall flat on our backs. Delusional,
As I create a vision, I return to the center of life,
Hopefully different next time around.

Auras spiritis in broomsticks to flee off.
Concaves of doom beckon in despair with deems aloofness.
Ripped inside walls to beckon boundaries astray.
Wretched amicable fathom mere lies
To deepen currents of hastening dews upon my character.
Warmth like hot-air in the midst of summer bitterness,
Breach down to heart with fury coldness.
That shriveling feeling rose from within,
Like twine once shrouded.
Splattered blood artistically devious,
Guilty hands unraveled for judgment,
Drew up a dread soul's portrait.
And t'was mine.

The anarchy that shredded a nostalgic grief
Bids me on a drift,
Approaching supremacy.
It is bitter, like sweet whiskers,
Proliferating indulgence,
Drained from a sober soul.
These bees-mead-o'er, outrageously demised,
Thereafter stagnated.
Rein your kingdom,
Reunite your priers.
Wretched old synagogues,
Probing degenerating blast,
For I'm the Sunway from the east,

My electrons indeed full of radiance.
Altered the venom,
From the demon,
Well on in mission,
To poison our fellow men.

Futile weakness prevails, undermined above the surface,
Manipulating and contradicting our self-completion,
Spoiling our perseverance in a fearing way,
Making us vulnerable to the visible appearance,
Blinding us to the unseen, hidden truth,
Like black magic behind those purple curtains,
But irony still prevails.
Synchronize our paths, step by step,
Until then, I will be in a "great" depression,
Not necessarily reliable to any so-called—
The dimension of my awareness,
As I faith for a better world and a better life,
My perceptions get the best out of me.
My concern worries me.
Self-reflection strikes inside of me, trying to get out,
Clarifying bumpy pathways, but for how long will it last?
Why is my nature unconsciously and forever probing my
Own self-degeneration?
Trying to force a sound, I suddenly start to glare,
Like a nervous arteries improperly functioning,
Nothing I said made sense,

In my perpetual search of comprehension,
I took a stand, finally made more than just a crunch—
Yelled instead: parallels work wonders, like opposites
attract.
That is our dimension tracking life into perspective.
Abide from that mud,
Clean your socks and walk away, holding your
Shoes on top of your head, because nothing needs to
make
Sense, or does it?

Another lullaby comes by,
Mercifully delivered. Sacred
to our hearth, gift from our supreme, but taken away by
demons. We need a comeback.
Warm breath, sweet whispers, danger approaches, making
us
Trip and fall. Take another chance: wipe out them shed
Tears, for there will be a new tomorrow, fresh from the
pot.
Stir it up slowly, enjoy presently.
Far, far away, we hear disturbance. Coffee spilled, but
We don't mind. Coming to knock in our door, strength
Become weakness. Light, dark. Heartaches. Mind versus
Imagination. Evils prevail, meanwhile the goods fade
away.
Grasped words are in equivalent to sentiments.

Hence that in some field of life
Where one does not belong,
Shall it not be,
Or one will perish.
Away must stay,
But far way will cherish
and will not go astray.
The battle of will,
Sorority of kill,
Not a flavor of love,
Who will survive?
He was not going to let go,
Not without a fight, not
This time, especially not in this life,
If you could just hold on
Tight, ours belong life.

A voice in my head telling me the pain is nonexistent; we
Think about it, but we don't have to accept it. The proverbs
Of life intrigue the capacity, triggering the curious eyes
In the midnight darkness. We tend to feed what we see
And carve it into ourselves. The lust to undermine others
In conjunction with self-centered persona, the result of
Many, many injustices and uncaring behaviors towards the
Well-being of our fellow man. This selfish act leads us to

Reckless decisions harmful to others in the aspect that
we
Have created self-observant personality.

Knife through the heart.
Wounded soul.
Feelings described
But not felt—
Rationalized instead.
Desires not met…
Vulnerability is your status,
Yet the pain is unavoidable.
Try to overcome it. We are calling.
Have courage
Yeah, that's it, courage!
Force a smile to the insanity
And ambiguity of a miscomprehended world.
Cloudy beginnings and bright endings. It might be.
Yeah, it's a way of life, but not "the" way.
Carried out by illumination, delusional, and coercive
forces,
What causes unpredictability?
Eternal peace is not in your domain,
Struggle is the pace that suffocates you,
Leveling inner growth to the infinite,
Elaborating life through a process far more complicated,
Acceptance mere distress, leaving me suspicious.

Nature's inheritance makes you a part of existence.
You are not alone, but we are alone;
Just a fragment filled with purpose bigger than our proportion.

Momentum,
Havoc the mimics,
Ecliptic,
Not charismatic,
Like a snow cascade
Glowing into a basket,
Proliferating indulgence.
Contemporaneous solutions,
Millenniums of confusions.
I gauged, exasperated.
Eyes didn't blink,
Couldn't believe my ears,
I stood still.
A miracle witnessed.
Suspended in the mid-air,
I came to find myself collapsing,
Then vanished in the higher air.
From afar small people murmur,
From above lights, glittering rumors.
The turmoil set me free.
My soul n' my body couldn't make up.
More time was conceived instead.

I shall indulge for better ways,
And aim for higher meaning.
My purpose in the earthly life,
A part of me will always remain.
Someday in the dark corners of universe,
Other times heavenly rejoicing.
White robes symbolizing peace found,
Blood washed from our entrances.
Marvelous creature,
Savoring new times of times.
Life goes on,
Since God pressed on,
Now, pause it, stop;
Forward or rewind it,
Perhaps save it or trash it,
(Humans manifestations)
Know thy track,
Where you want it.
Pour out some wine,
In a slow- mid-set beat,
Listen to your life,
And let it roll with the flow.

An endeavor that swings its magical wand.
Like by a trickster when others are lured.
Man's hardship woven society's pain,
Drinking mere violence.

Trying in vain, reasoning,
There's no getting through the core.
Proliferating indulgence against thee,
Breaking Somme's heels,
for there's too much heed,
merging from the creed.

Man's railroads are sterile.
From bickering one shall apart,
Spare to be dissipated,
Refuse to dive into this bloodshed.
For I wish to die in peace,
Inculpable of manslaughter,
Trying to catch my breath,
I've been hurt,
In this battle of survivors.
I'm putting down my sword,
And grabbing a pen.

As I walk in the battlefield of life,
People throwing their spectrum at me,
Hitting my armor, but falling down.
As I lean over my shoulder, no worries, I keep on walking with my
Head up, like a hero in a war zone.
There's not a turning point.
Can't break my spirit.

Just tingle feelings.

What's an enigma?

Everything so easy in the surface and mysterious beneath.

I chose, only a few,

Almost timeless under the sun.

Before dark comes, what are you going to do at the dawn?

Today you plan, tomorrow you realize, and on, looking back,

what good does it? The future? Already passed, for time

is infinite, looking way ahead of you, yesterday made

no sense. The future of the human race is one of a kind.

Togetherness was.

Abomination to the forsaken soul,

Emerging to the surface,

Trying communicating with our mind.

Message disturbed along the way.

Trying to understand it, in vain.

Should I give it a time? Even more time, perhaps?

Therefore, I started bleeding inside;

In my search for the still, remains unknown,

I burn low.

Like justice, the core of life,

But reality, so upset.

Life still is a mystery, not a concept.

We know nothing but futileness.

Hurried to be buried in our own disgrace
We....we....who are we?
Mystery might be,
But fight we must,
Together, to survive to live on,
Now, I hope,
One day we'll see that child again,
And justice will be just.

Hang on tight, don't let nothing bounce you off your
Saddle, and if they do? Get right back on that horse.
"Falling down standing up,"
Because the end of the line is suppress by the time
Captivated in the game of life
Then released into divine
As a wish of fulfillment
Watery eyes turn into crystal, as if magic.
Deep breath, eyes close, imagination runs wild.
Remember...one day you will smile again.

When doth life!

Broken heart. Whose? Could be anyone; a close friend, a family member, or perhaps yourself. When one's heart is broken, there's going to be some "grief," along with the pressure felt to hold it in. A heart when broken it doesn't tell you how long it'll be hurt. It can be temporary; some last for a long period of time, say years, and dealing with a broken heart is frustrating. Some people tend to suppress what they are feeling, trying to hold it in.

Being strong by not permitting yourself to feel the pain might not be the best approach sometimes. Like many believe, sometimes is appropriate to have some emotional release and get it out of your system, because repressing your feelings can be harmful, both physically and emotionally. It is far healthier to release your emotions.

To do that, sometimes you have to talk with someone. Conversation can be a good way of releasing the pain that you are feeling. Shakespeare wrote in Macbeth, "Give sorrow words; the grief that does not speak whispers the o'er-fraught heart and bids it break."

So talk to someone who will listen to you; a true friend to whom you can describe what you're feeling can makes you understand better, and therefore, you have a better way of dealing with them. And who knows? Maybe the other person went through same experience and perhaps give you comfort that is more practical. But talking is not the only way to express your feelings, for some don't like to talk about them. Finding a way to communicate, either by writing or talking can relieve a lot of the pressure of the pain that's crushing your soul.

You can choose to be strong and have your feelings bottled up inside of you, or you could get them out of you, sometimes releasing them. Crying can make the process quicker. Don't feel ashamed. Let your tears be shed.

The bible says there is "a time to weep." Shedding the tears of a broken heart can be sometimes be a part of the healing process. But of course, everyone deals with pain in different ways.

We have to remember that we don't have much control over what others do, but we have control over ourselves and our emotions. First, we need to know what we should let into our mind and thoughts. Think positive always, no matter what. Don't you have any faith? How bad can it be?

Sometimes we get so caught up in what we can't do that we forget what we can or are supposed to do. Let not our circumstances paralyze our lives. We should be moving forward.

If we let that happen, our problems and circumstances will be in control of our lives. Instead of being paralyzed, we can use the situation to our advantage. Even though it's not easy, we should try hard and learn how to cope with badness such as a broken heart with good situation, like being reasonable with ourselves.

Sublimeness

Sublime compassion as my companion.
Conscious awareness to bind such magnitude.
Trend to the trades'
Ambiguous momentum,
Anonymous perceptions,
Felt upon mind,
Cruel to the eyes like broken glass,
Fury unbearable to the flesh.
Crying out loud, nobody listens.
Contemporary solutions drift in confusion and pain.
Pillows talk, bed moaning,
Conjunction, together, rise.
Words of consolation cure a wounded soul,
Darkness brings hope, ironically,
Submission to unfulfilled desires,
What a bliss to the controversy bless?
Supremacy inwards rebelled, nature rewards blindly
Chaos to the surface, or just peace to deaths,
Refuse to the just.
Step aside and don't crumble.

Again enchanting beautifully that Pasadena.
Like a blossoming lily of the valley
Shivering thy shrew.

Two eyes have met for the first time, but very familiar,
Reflecting a distant life.
Pondered gratitude and yet can't seem to figure it out.
Excuse me, but I've seen those before.
-You...? Am I...?
Glimpse away in desperation, Rutland cry for help. Why?
Deep sigh, embrace as default.
Tinkering mind mislead the essence to perfection.
Misguided, I might say. My lord, it's a torch.
Old bedtime stories forgotten. Hidden mysteries lay
Everywhere, unprovoked misfortune. Innocent
entrepreneur,
Equivalent rewards taped as you rifted way.
No time for this parade of charades.
I have a time to catch, for it's here.
I will be seeing you around.

Resemble

Here I began my last words with my last paragraphs.

By the end, I started.

When I'm done, this pain shall die away.

The beginning lies ahead,

So I grabbed these next lines,

Of what a pain feels, what a pain does.

Pain suppressed by a greater pain.

Pain cures pain.

Courage, fear, AND pain, life's primarily burdened trios,

Walking large on the sea of my being.

Fear and the pressure to hold the pain.

How long, mo? I moaned.

Does the absence of pain, make a life vain?

Is a sick yet alienated Heart inequevalent to a broken hearth?

My heart pounds with questions.

My mind beats desperately,

Till the greatest pain,

But "Courage is fear holding on a minute longer,"

Continuously consumed by little pain.

Live as I wish.

Use and abuse,

But because no one will go unpunished,

Thou I shall lose,

Dost thou perish
Life portraits confuse...
It's no one's fault but my own.
As life goes on,
And the world moves on,
Seemingly, I can't go on,
Nor move on.
I'm on my own,
Not knowing, what's going on.
Perhaps I should hold on, till is on.
Trying to reach out, no one will hear me out,
I felt left out of the crowd. I shouted, Crying out loud?
Wouldn't help out! Therefore, I'm staying out.

He who's mastering her wants,
Like with a magic wand.
She vowed to agree.
Rather than happiness she seek,
She weeps mere lust of the heart.
Her frigidity to be hardened,
He that secretly plot against all goods abound,
Corpse embodiment he put lying 'round.

We bubble forth with prejudice.
Charm our way out of justice.
The double-heartbeat-pace,
From a commonplace to a broken place.

Insider's rage beckons to ploy.

One that gathers smiles for decoy.

Thereafter bring forth shame,

But from memories, it shall soon fade.

Dreams ripped anight's darkens.

Deflected reason with faultiness of trueness.

In my innermost parts I wonder,

That my offset heart lingers to suffer.

In my universe of words,

I would drown all the pain in the world.

Now let us hope

That no sanctuary hence in order to console.

When life's not in sync,

We see the color of sin,

The sound of poetry,

And the folkloric symphony, fading out slowly,

Like smoke in the air, ravishingly twisting.

Include the echo of solitude,

The rhythms of words,

The unit of blood,

The melancholy of music,

Adjusters of the mystic,

The awareness of existence.

The end of line,
Suppress by the time,
Embraced with deep sigh,
In the game of life,
Emerging from the depths of our heart,
In the midst of consciousness, it transpired.
The history of questions,
Final destination,
Nobody seems to know,
The weight of our souls.
Man's reality,
Is like the theory of relativity,
Adds up everything,
You end up with the same thing.
Perhaps a few more flinch.

Life's full of lessons,
Indeed, life is learning.
Useful preparation for upcoming tests.
I giggle nervously.
I even worried, disoriented.
How did I do?
I did my best, but
I don't know who is to judge?
Thy sentences
Determinate by ones like me?
Oh, the remedy!

I don't need the test, just give me my lessons.
I shall learn as I wish, use them,
If cometh to that,
Not as surviving skills,
Just amusements and delights.
Fulfilling hungry curiosity
And thirsty consciousness.
I even express them in the empty room,
But not to the ears, for there were none.
Message deliberately
was not delivered.
The reason why
Confusion arises:
Just thought for myself.

My trueness
Is a willful heart,
Architecting my happiness
In deflecting faultiness,
As the drunkard evildoers flee off.
I shake off my sins of deems.
Instinctively unmasking mere accolades,
I play fair, and I'm bound for status quo,
And make no sound against the grain.
If I so speak senselessly,
I'd place a gag in my devilish way.
But I rather aim with a voice of truce,

For it will set me free.
When I sought with my innermost concerns,
I believe I have the answer:
Not in my commonplace,
But in the gist afar.
I move straightforwardly with steadiness,
Until I feel whole and complete,
For I do not poke the unknown,
Nor to make a plight of it,
But simply know, existence itself.
With a voice of truce,
For it will set me free

Rather than tomorrow's sorrow
We often sow,
Is embracing today's sin
With a positive spin

In the multitude of everyday queries,
I approach every moment of tribulation
Like a child on Christmas morning.
I dream, make wishes, and hope.
Closely I follow life's path,
Walking hand-to-hand,
Driven life by destiny.

Oh, How futile and oh, how lofty! Would it be!
Not wanting nothingness,
Only foul to feed.
Easily I let go, I forget in purpose,
And eagerly I forgive,
The burdens of life,
Reversed
In these verses.
Hollowed it today in a sweet melody.

lost a-lone 'n all
In times of time
Reminiscing in times lost,
Unsearchable n' untouchable.
Perpetually buried in our subconscious being.
Trying defying a lost purpose,
Like once undoubtedly hath missed,
The unknown questioned thine born,
Became known-ed for its secrecy.
There's time when I'm alone,
The air withdrew in disarray within me
Begging time to return;
I timed waiting.

"O" sound of the infinity,
Martyr of marvels pulling wools,
In a city constantly brewing,

New fads, new tales, or just new crazes.

The womb that never seems to fed up.

How's and whys does not Savior.

Pour another revolution,

The end is now here,

To times anew.

lost a-lone 'n all,

in times of time.

Drunken Child whispered to me,

"O'phat the honey."

I witnessed then, running, stumbling, and wobbling

Down to the fumbling, deserted street's corridors.

As the evildoers passersby,

Handing out baits,

Why do we parch in your jest?

Call upon the redeemers from time afar,

Alleviation of a sober soul,

For no longer, we shall seek vexation,

But repentance,

And our sins to be forged.

Forgiveness, thy Father, frivolously we beg.

As in all things truly worthwhile in life,

We nail our knees in rocks washed in blood,

The bloodguilt of what's real,

As a symbol of sacrifice and tragedy caused

The pain and suffering to fade.

And the deceased held in our arms,
Refusing to let go, but we must.
The Crippled Spirit acting treacherously,
Trying to be strong,
"We let go and let God deal with it,"
Because the "pain really never goes away."

Just one more day to live.
One more day to die.
A loving, dying life.
Can't contain our fortitude of prejudice.
In limitation, meditation of mind-extension.
To measure up and pursue the search of a meaning.
To reinvent what life doth upon.
To lay under and fondle a blueprint zest in ash.
Life dost doth perish indeed,
And death dies forever,
In a seemingly reversed puzzle,
And parallels ambiguity, yet one can't pertain without
another.
For a cause sowed boastfully and bountifully profound,
To mend what's bent,
And to be what was meant.

Sonnets

———◆———

Beyond the obvious and the naked eye, laid a foundation,
A purpose squirmed to be fulfilled.
To live the greatest story ever told,
Where no ostracized jinx brier in what we shared,
For being the Shareholders of our own dreams,
Life doth bestow us,
Heretofore, in the battlefield of life,
The little pawns acting reckless, protecting the fort,
Make yet greater kings,
And take no promises for granted,
Such as "do" "me and thee consummate we."

To "do" "me and thee consummate we,"
O'phat the honey of my sweetness,
Angel sent from heavens upon,
To brighten up my daunt days,
To lift me up when I'm down,
My goddess, your trueness,
Come to me now, your lovely one.
Love me now, and loath me not.
Come, come.
Your humble virtues, my epiphany,

The rode models of sisterhood.
Without you, I'm helpless 'n hopeless.
No man is worthy of your beauty.
Everything I've dreamed of.
Every wish I hoped for to fruition rose.
I'm addicted to this love,
And love I found.

Paired in the arctic place.
Between light and time, laid will,
The Queen and I,
Complete they feel.
Life, they brought to light,
Stride, they fought to quibble.
Forever thinking the hues,
And together feeling the blues.
Like "The heavens for height and the earth for depth,"
Such is my heart for you.
Thy vows I, girded for evermore, to thee.

She was enslaved amongst their peers,
Shuffle up and rigid,
In the multitude of obnoxious queries.
Dealt right to left in circles.
She lay, astonished, as with a glazing red in the middle.
Needn't to be rescued,
For it was all for one.

Options narrowed to nothingness.
I played a fasted hand to forthright my faultiness,
But in kings heart her bejeweled woven in disarray.

Your mastery experience has owned up your quantum majesty.
If you can take it and fake it,
Exude your ethereal glow to cover up a "rotten hand,"
Rely on luck, fate, and the cycles of life.
Leave the ways open, and play to win,
Anything is possible.
You won't know till you try.
Will you consider defeated in a single hand,
Or deal over?
Or will you throttle in a Russian roulette game and focus under fire?
The game has taken an ugly spew,
Once you had thrown your hat in.
The results are still up in the air,
There are not definite answers or definite time.
Move accordingly to bend what's real.
Draw it up in a mind game,
If I so speak in a hundred tongues, let me intrude.
Do you burn out playing?
Or fade away, defeated?
I, myself believe you'd come around as a survival,
If I've know you.

Your eloquence adds persuasiveness to your lips.
To inspire another,
Teach one, and then call the bluff.
With a house full of hearts,
Deuce becomes mightier than aces.
Do you play one hand, and or with both?
One hand washes the other vigilantly.
Do I fold before your goddess ways?
Or like a fool, head-on, driven by fate?
Will the deck strike back fury, spinning unbearably?
If I hold my queen of hearts close to my heart,
will my chances rise up to momentum?
I'll keep playing your worthy adversary.
With fair play. "Beggars can't be choosers."
Deal another, and I shall act upon it.
Or game over!

In my deepest dream,
A picture in black and white,
Wobbling, fast-furious in the hollow wind.
A naked woman
Stumbling down the dusty, deserted corridors.
Dost vanish in the dark lights.
Campaigned by only monstrous pillars,
And the echo of her footsteps.
Make'm come alive.
"I am asleep, but my heart is awake.

There is the sound of my dear one knocking!"
The serpent has once more returned,
For a final bite.
From my innermost part, it stirs up contentions.
Why do I cause to anger, dear one?
The pain felt realer as the dream wore off.
Now I'll fix my robe upon you,
And lay under your garments,
And you shall raise your matrix.
Because flesh by flesh,
Soul for soul
And blood for blood,
I'm here to resgate your life with mine.
You will inherit life,
And we shall too overcome.

To open the "secret chamber",
And access the heart's portal,
Or the "labyrinthine" entryways,
One must be destined.
The code within minds can be comely unraveled,
And the passageway of the starry heart's vault be reached.
Head upon shoulder, rest with surety.
Allow our Animagus to come out
And your "Diva-tude" to dance freely
To the rhythm of my heartbeat

At the pedestal of happiness.

If perhaps, my imagination can't pertain your godlessness,
I beg pardon to thee.
I shall instead contain your kindness,
For you speak in an agreeable tone,
And love you awake in me.
My consistency upon you exclusively,
Sealed upon my heart indefinitely.
For "love is as strong as death is."
I shall then, thy (die) loving you,
And love till'death.

Now that the impasse has passed,
The chase and excitement has wandered out,
Will you play in an unknown gist?
Between rolling the dice cube for luck,
Flipping cards with mannerisms,
To check "a" mate for partnership,
Or winning the joker for triumph;
I'd wish for my queen,
On a roller strike.
Will you delight me, a hand on the table, as I?
Colloquially lay down my precious vessels to your droves,
To atone what was once curbed and concealed.
The queen's flipside is "tres" bizarre.

From the lattice of my imagination,
I glimpse over to see happiness.
I believe a part of me touches it.
Happiness is a myth invented by a coveting man.
I might have dreamed about it here and then,
But my heart-knocks, awakens me to real-I-tears.
Like dead I'm unconsciously happy,
For they don't fear.
Uncanny we seek.
Pressure and stress fraught to mend.
Endangers life for thrill.
Moments of euphoria and ecstasy plowed the devil in me.
I remain neutral in the midst of this polarity of vulgarity.
For being neither happy or unhappy,
I'm indifferent to my emotions.
Balancing my Gemini.
The unconscious happy of me,
And the conscious "unhappy" me;
The twin that never separates.
For not being happy does not make me unhappy.

Went round and flattered,
To measure up a dread derided soil.
To wordily flourish a concubine soul.
Watered some Epic seeds in the centerpiece of me.
To beautify and personify my persona's heart,
Enchanting euphemism heads on shoulder,

Floating lightly and delicately in midair of the west side.
I induce breath upwardly north.
And, in east I was
Looking to the south-side river-crossed bridge.
I was pulled by the hollow wind midstream.
Stormily coming home,
In the wind of change.

"The" Spirit

Call me mischievous;
Pioneer of time,
The essence of existence-endings.
Sough unclear…
The word and its prerogative,
The melancholic entrepreneurs of me,
And "world" its dilemmas.
Loneliness's companion,
Enthralled beneath our doors,
Embedded,
Then released,
Euphorically transpire.
Let life be taken by life,
Driven your opposing.
A journey of unknowns,
The ecstasy of a moment,
Faded in one's troubled soul.
I see it in your eyes.
Speak with your divine,
For I am the same flesh,
Am too being corrupted.
Mercy shall be upon us.

What a benevolent gesture,
Within essentiality!

Then today I saw a fascinating star activity.
Downward on earth,
HUMAN BEING.
More than galaxies,
From our DNA to life experienced,
Conjures up to the infinite stars.
Each one of us more than mere planets,
More often is our conscience,
Aware of itself,
With a flick to our subconscious,
We're the earth-movers.
We push it into the infinite space,
Round and square into the infinite time,
'Till we reach another dimension,
We conquer the unknowns part of the universe.

From beliefs to practice, we survive indefinitely,
Human race never into extinction.
We make the universe what it;
We change beyond measurements.

The oak tree may outlive individuals,
But the human race has been cloned permanently.
The Evil and the Goods battle over us,

Ultimately, the choice is ours.
I ask you raise your hands up high,
If you are feeling human.
A proud being,
For we constitute both physical and spiritual worlds,
solely.
We get great pleasure in pleasuring,
Reason why we attract attention,
But we choose to devote ourselves,
To the one and the only God,
Our creator and of all things,
To our disposition,
I thank my lord for he has made me a human.

But what a critical time,
Modern time has become!
Indeed, hard times to deal with
We dwell on.
Protect our fort we must,
Not with weapons of destruction,
But with hope we surrender ourselves,
Choosing our battles carefully,
For life's not a game of poker.
We hold onto our chips,
Nonetheless shan't fold.
Where "the pen becomes mightier than the sword,"
Avoiding being dissipated,

And crying in dissolution.
The failures we anticipated,
Against our worthy adversary.
We keep pushing,
'till the gate of impasse passed,
Through our fingertips,
And the footprints abandoned.
To a new era,
Peace of mind,
And peace for all and good.

But it is the Night that is my favorite.
The Son of divine,
Came in a light,
Filled with delights.
Set up his tent on the outside,
Candlelight bursting all night,
Before your eyes.

My own retribution has been lifted.
Your hearts lurking shall not,
But goods are sought.
For God has put on the show.
The birds might not be singing,
But the angels are whistling clarinets,
And blowing trumpets.
Meanwhile the stars are

dancing around the moon,
And the sky's adornments
Have been hanged,
Like the Christmas tree,
And I'm the baby,
Son of God.

The dying night,
Nature touches you at its best.
Imagination at its peek,
And the beginning of a new day.
The horizon is asleep.
Differences are channeled.
The sun in you has risen.
Shall let's not partake,
For it's still young.

What doth life!

How would life be in the ultimate phase of happiness and completion? How would life be when there's no more struggles and hurdles, just joy and happiness? But perhaps most importantly, what's your purpose in this life? What does life mean to you?

Occasionally we all might have asked these questions, questions like, what's the meaning of life? Can humans be able to lead a perfect life ever? And if so, how would it be? As you see, question are all the time arising. Confusion and mysteries remain beneath the surface.

Does life has a meaning, or this is it? No mysteries, no great accomplishment? Just the mundane: taking care of the family, traveling and sustaining the basics? Your curiosity somehow "lethargic," embracing life with just common sense, not looking for more? The quotidian seems to do it for you, and you're quite happy with the status quo without scrutinizing. You are comfortable, and that's your concept about the meaning of life.

Some have a triggering mind "curiosity" that constantly demands them to dig more, to search, to investigate, and perhaps to find a new and better meaning of life and cultivate talents that give them a role to play in the scene of life. What is their purpose? What are they here for? And so the search begins: the search that most of us are doing, the search for the meaning of life—the meaning of life in general, and the meaning of you being here. Nevertheless, it is to say, the search often engage in is to pursue and lead a happy life. So I ask, what doth life?

People's search for the meaning of life is often expressed through them in arts, music, science, and things that feel satisfaction. It's like understanding your soul and expressing it to others in a clearest way possible. You try to photocopy your soul and mind, but how clear is it? How authentic is it? The authenticity of that copy is in how people see you, but they can never see as clearly as you see yourself. Only a blurry photocopy is what at least they can see, but the stronger your ability or talent to expressed yourself through whatever, the clearer people will be able to see you.

Life! Is it just eighty years? If so, then why do we want to know about billions of years ago and billions of years to come? It's like our physical structure is not in harmony with our perpetual heart, our infinite brain capacity, or everlasting soul.

Why do we die, what happens when we do, and where do we go? Is there an afterlife? Are the dead conscious? Is there a burning hell and heaven? Are there other creatures in other parts of the universe? Why are we here? For what? What's our destination, why do we pursue happiness? How do we pursue happiness? Why is my mind forever probing my own degeneration? Do I search for the unknown with my curious eyes? Is it just mingling curiosity doomed to fade out but make us a little bit more interesting to ourselves and others, but with no lasting purpose, just superficiality?

Endless questions. Will we ever know? Endless questions. Endless questions. But I have to ask. I can't live with a starving curiosity. Is the question whether we are to feed what we see and what we want to know? Our mind is a conscious one, for it, too, is aware of its own self-existence, asking itself the same darn question, while it takes a spin into the city to feed that "old gray mattress."

All your actions and questions are a self- recycling operation—for what reason? I myself named it something: "Self-ma-tic."

Endless questions. You'll return in a billion years, so you can ask the same endless questions. Who knows?

As life seems to go on, everybody is caught up doing their mimics, their acts, and their dances, in music, arts, and expression. In trying and struggling, life gets the best out of every one of us, no one excluded. We worry and we live, trying our best for our own amusement, fulfillment, and satisfaction. Why we do what we do? It's only a human remark; that's what's different and separates us from the rest vast universe.

The human race is a very special one, and in its best

moments, it's magnificent, with such an indiscreet magnitude.

Are you familiar with words like beauty, love, wisdom, perfection, and happiness? If so, my friend, that's what's human. That's what our race is all about. We need to stay focused and cultivate our best qualities for our favors and their offspring.

The glimpse of agony from the realization upon our minds in contradiction with our souls is often uncomfortable for our inner peace. Imagining ourselves with nonexistent answers we seek in the darkest moment of our life, we still we don't know if it hurts or hunts us, but we don't want to leave anything behind, struggling and not knowing where exactly we're heading. It's a vague subject. Confusion is a mist; the cause of this powerful motivation makes it seem like we are divided and deprived, incapable not just of the quotidian, but of something very mysterious behind all this majesty, I believe that pushes us ahead to this strange field of life, leaving us nowhere even to begin to comprehend it. You can just close your eyes and try to picture it to relieve yourself. Imagination. If I could be where my mind is! It's a beautiful thing that only resides inside each one of us in probably different aspects. We manifest uniquely, which therefore make us what we are.

This distinctive element of nature is where nothing is concrete and nothing is for sure. Look for the absolute:

what is it? What's the ultimate? Is there an end to our curiosity, our understanding, and our learning?

We struggle along the way to try and find the truth, but we must know. We want to know. The question is, will we ever know? If so, when will we know it? Until then, let's just keep doing what we do. Is this really important? Is this necessary? We often find ourselves asking the same question over and over, and one of the most common questions is, why is everything the way it is?

We can't change reality, but when it hits us, you wonder, and it hurts not knowing the mysteries of life—the suffering and the outer world. Have you ever wondered what's out there or how it is? You anticipate the end, becoming anxious, and some actually give up, claiming we should be happy with what we are and with what we have—the status quo.

You fantasize. You almost live it by trying turning it into reality that is very often different. Whom are we kidding? One thing is for sure: it's so amazing that it make us find a piece of that hidden source that can be manifested just in part in our daily life. We are not the main reason for this life. We are not the center of life, as if we live to serve somebody else, somebody bigger, better, and holier than us.

To begin with an exceptional, non-profit manifestation to acquire a most privileged yet anatomical prospect, enable yourself to conquer our deepest, most desirable expectation. Combined with reflection of the smallest, satisfying thing, a glimpse, into the nonfiction part of the world, it's rather exquisite. Engaged in a more powerful kind of "personated," very ambiguous encryption in not just our soul, but also in our mind, corrupted by this day-to-day "mumbo-jumbo" if I might say, but hey, another human story comes by and you either like it, accept it, you criticize it and move on, because another episode is about to air. At last, we stand as if nothing has changed.

Self-Reflection

A well-developed person is consisting upon a vast range of self-determination and the ability to "straddle" opponents whenever you have a crossed the paths needed in your advancement, not necessarily harmful to others, constantly rebuilding and changing as we go, meeting others' expectations, at least a strategy is more like it.

One's character is to reassure personal limitation and the preparation for the strange field of life: where you are, who you represent, whether you are to be accepted by the outside world or know where you stand, people-wise. In your enduring self-awareness, you should not get lost in the mist, scrounging yourself like a paper in a heavy wind. You are the master of your own destiny.

Everybody occasionally needs a reality-check to remind ourselves of the things we neglect, the things we postpone when the circumstance is due, and of the unpredictability forging life astray, creating confusion and thus limiting one's achievement. Perhaps blood is "thicker than water," but it wouldn't be blood if it wasn't for water, same as for people without other's collaboration per se (whom are we showing our works to?)

To define, you have first to refine, accessing methods

available and the tools as your accessories to get your "tickets." Learn how to use these tools and that will serve as your passport in this world for your final destination.

I say life is a semi-automatic. If you walk the straight-arrow line with balance, with no seesaw or zigzag, but focus instead on the straight path of life with courage, patience, and self-determination, in the end, everything will go in your favor if you just hang on tight and let no one bounce you off your saddle. Keeping your faith won't be less important, for the strategy is for your own happiness, and it was, too, given to you. The key is to know when to let go and when not to, for what's is worth.

Least but not last, believe in the purpose of life as the cure of all illness, even if you have to restrain yourself in determining the "accuracy" that you've mapped for, but taken away by the harsh reality often dissolute, for the victims can too be winners. Always keep your head up, not dignifying the adversary that's there calumniating against one's self. Who's the man to cause you affliction?

There's nothing in this world that will harm you if you believe in yourself.

It seems in life that we can never win as we go picking up pieces left from our dissolute reality, trying constantly to rebuild ourselves and perhaps mold ourselves into a new self-persona with a new perspective in life, new concepts, and new ideas. The hustling is endless, since we can never stop looking for more ventures. Life's beyond achievement:

contemplating and rejoicing at times, struggling and hustling often, with a handful of hurdles. Does it give us strength, or does it weaken us? At least that's how it looks every now and then, but do not be alarmed or discouraged.

There are just bigger things than us in life that are always up for a disappointment. This is cruel reality. Battling our way up against nature, we're defeated, or is it just bad nature? The key is to pick up the most pieces you can and keep up, and not give up. Avoiding spreading yourself too thin. Hopefully we're able to rebuild ourselves again, for the old ways got you broken. Unfortunately, so will this one— only take it easy this time. Maybe you won't hit yourself so hard. A word of advice: you won't even feel the fall.

Don't feed in into it. Nothing is definite; everything comes and goes. How strong are you? Are you willing to let go when necessary, without crushing yourself? There's an expression, "Learn when to fold and when to hold" just the right amount. Because just like a temporary shadow, everything will disappear. Take nothing as if it is forever, because you will lose it, and you set yourself for another disappointment. Remember, you need to start over and never give up, knowing that is the way of life. Why all the commotion? Didn't you know it was meant to happen? Don't fool yourself. Be reasonable, for you have no superpowers, but you're acting like the creator. Perhaps can you defy death?

The only thing left is what has always been: our everlasting faith, somehow prolonged. Life is still not a losing battle, for it take patience and lots of courage to not give up, and keep our dreams as real as possible. My friend, it doesn't matter how many times you have fallen; pick up the pieces, regroup, and keep on going. One day you will get there, and all the hurdles shall be forgotten. For what's it was worth, you did it.

Life as a Stage

Sure, we are all thrilled with science's discoveries in many areas of technology, medical advancements, and such, but we are also aware that a thousand years ago we didn't have any of these new technologies, discoveries, and luxuries, and yet people managed to live healthier, and perhaps happier lives.

The question is, do we really need all these "great" new advancements? Or do we have them for other reasons? One thing I'm sure of: it's amazing. Human beings, acting at their best it can be the most beautiful and magnificent creational designs. But sometimes we take it all the wrong way, with our manifestation and reactions to anger, along with our mimics, our humor, our thoughts, our feelings, our minds, our hearts, our judgment, our critiques of one another, our absence, and our unawareness of things we don't know or understand.

We are humans, we are what we are, and we do things the way we do. Sure, some are born more talented than others and have more skills such as in areas of language and communication, but what do we know? Sometimes what we think is better for us might turn out to be quite the opposite. Let's not take what we have or know for granted and undermine those less fortunate. Hopefully someday we all are on the same page, where there we will no longer judge one and another, living in peace and harmony.

This is not just a fantasy, but a purpose set in our heart since the beginning of time. when we laughed through our mistakes and embarrassment, knowing that we are just trying to be happy, even when we pick the wrong path. Someday we are going to realize that we are all the same, and that we should bear with our fellow man. The world has changed and so has man. We shouldn't let the events of things change us, but we should change them. What's more important? As I'm saying, it's about humans surviving through times, and our mission not just during our earthling lifetime, but after life as well. Can we ever be sure about anything? Will we ever agree on what's really best for everyone?

Things changes with time, and that's what makes it hard to have one fixed theory about something: nothing is definite. Nothing is absolute. They will simply change and be different. The key is to be able to be as flexible and changeable as possible in order to be up to date. Perhaps the universe is a conscious being, changing accordingly to its metabolism, making it impossible to understand it. In the other hand, the universe itself is not aware of its own events. Nobody knows when, where, how, and why; we just don't know. The deep questions still go on.

The matter of the truth is no longer important. What

used to be common now is very uncommon, because we decide the wrong to the right based on our own wishes and fulfillment and our own desires. Long story short: people now are self-centered, haughty, stubborn, and selfish. Indeed this is a very critical time for men. A bible passage tells us, "In the last days, critical times hard to do deal with will be here. For men will be lovers of themselves, lovers of money, self-assuming, haughty, blasphemers, disobedient to parents, unthankful, disloyal, having no natural affection, not open to any agreements, slanders, without self control, fierce, without love of goodness, betrayers, headstrong, puffed up with pride, love of pleasures rather than lovers of God, having a form of godly devotion but proving false to its power."

As far as I'm concerned, I aim to be free more than anything, meaning that I want to be in control of my life, because life is the only place we can express ourselves and do our acts, in many ways. I believe that wisdom comes first, and once you have found it, you will be a reasonable person, capable of understanding ourselves and another, and our surroundings.

You hear a lot of theories and stories everyday from all kind of sources but who's telling the truth? That is why you have to go behind the "scenes" of life and find out for yourselves rather than accepting it blindfolded. That makes you create some kind of identity based on lies, and there you are, heading toward harmful indulgence. Without realizing it, your life is on the line. You start to look at things based on those previous lies, making unrealistic judgments and make-believe, and so on. The paradox is within you and yourself, but when encountering new things or people, where will you stand when proven false to everything you've had cultivated in your heart? Erasing them sure won't be easy, so being flexible and adaptable and, of course, open-minded is just a way of looking at things in life, so cultivate the good things in your heart, because you won't be taking anything with you.

We either blend into the reality we face or disappear in our fantasies, but we still don't lose the grip of our existence and our involvement in God's beautiful creation. We are a part of all this, and each one of us has a role at hand. We are waiting play it in order to teach, discipline, give courage, or just simply cheer another up when lost in the abundance of its disgrace. But we should put these uncertainties aside and think positively, even when we don't really know what we are doing—just that we are doing it with good intentions. Sometimes we don't play our role the way we are destined. For many reason we fall short. But If we wait and prepare ourselves for the destined role, we'd probably pull it off, and in some far, far land someone might have heard about it. He didn't jump off that bridge, because he stopped and listened, and it was good. Now he, too, is waiting and preparing for his time; maybe not to save a life, but to just to make life brighter and more entertaining for someone.

I believe there's good in everyone. We are reflection of God, made his image, and his fragments that will never go into extinction. Someday we will live forever in peace, harmony, and abundance.

None of this you see now will be anymore, except the good, so what's to worry? This is just a glimpse of the true real life that's yet to come. It's a simple test where we all know the answer, and still sometimes rebel against answer it right. Most of us have been misguided by our enemy, who has corrupted out minds with temptation that has led to destruction and death.

What is a man to accomplish in such a short span of life—only eighty years? It has been proven that our brain is in harmony with the purpose of an everlasting life. it would be a waste not to use it in 100 percent of our brain, we only use about 0.001 percent of 1 percent. Now imagine how smart we'd be if we could use just one full percent or just one-one-hundredth. I'm not even saying 2percent, and I'm not even thinking about 100 percent. Other theories suggest that we use 10 percent of our brain's full potential. That remains a mystery, even among the most intelligent people on earth. Man's learning is a long process, but it includes faith, belief, and knowing that life has a bigger and better meaning that is beyond our comprehension. To me this is common sense, which can go a long way together with common courtesy. That's, of course, a much more complicated subject to dwell on in areas like science of all kinds, like history, mathematics, and physics. Aren't we all curious to know, to invent, to create, and to be the first to solve a quantum-physics problem?

Well here's just a little reflection: the ability to manage the subconscious mind to prevent a non-existential, yet unpreventable situation , I would say we fear many things that yet we probably wont live to see.

Scientists believe that the human brain is the most complicated and the most complex object in the universe. In the brain there are about fifty billion neurons with a quadrillion synapses, or connections, with the capacity of operation of maybe ten quadrillion times per second. Just to compare, the most sophisticated computer has maybe 0.001 percent of the mental capacity of a fly. Comparing that with human brain is absurd. Unlike computers, the brain is capable of adjusting, programming, and "fixing" itself.

You might have heard the expression "use it or lose it," but it's not just an expression, for the human brain can change according to how you use or abuse it. There are two main factors that seem to determine how the brain evolves during our lifetime: what we let into our brain through our senses, and our choice of thoughts. Although some genes might influence mental development, the brain is not a fixed organ.

Let's see some of this wonderful operation happening in human brain. The brain is a very mutable and flexible organ, in constant change, not only through day-to-day experience. The way we think, also affects it. It's proven that mentally active people have 40 percent more synapses than those who aren't, concludes neurology. If you don't use it, you are going to lose it. There are some indications that we lose some brain cells, as we get older, but in a smaller proportion than we had thought before.

The human brain is divided in five main parts. First is the frontal lobe. Brain studies show that we use this part of the brain when we think about a word or memories, this part characterizes us for being what we are. The second part, the prefrontal cortex, is responsible for formulating thoughts, and connecting more with intelligence, motivation and personality. This part is mostly what distinguishes humans from animals. Behind the prefrontal cortex, there's a part called motor cortex. In there, billions of neurons connect with muscles. This area gives us our exceptional capacity of using our hands and using our mouth, lips, tongue, and facials muscle when we talk. The fourth is called Broca's area, which is responsible for the articulation of words and how we express them. We must know a language and the meanings of words, and that's where the final area of the brain ,called the Wernicke's area, comes in. It is where billions of cells work to translate words, both speaking and in writing. It is useful in learning a new language, for example.

As we see, the brain is a very complex organ that separates us from animals in other areas, such art and beauty, appreciation for music, moral values, in thinking and planning for the future, and for asking questions. There's more details in everything mentioned here such as communication, intelligence, memory, language and more processes of the human brain.

When a non-substantial element is encrypted in a problematic manner in our conscious mind, it's as a new factor that compels our decisions. But how can that be? I say that we think in miniature, but expressing it is much more difficult. We can only do so much, just a "glimpse"—after all, as humans, we feel and think we deserve much more than confusion, pain, and suffering. We need something better, happier, longer lasting, and more secure. We wish to be all as one as equals, but what happens when we fail and fall down, incapable. With all the negativity, we become less radiant.

This process within us is magnificent—finding ourselves questioning our existence constantly, avoiding hitting that brick wall. Human beings are contemplating the cosmos less and less. We want to rethink things in the green rim and take pleasure in meeting new acquaintances as we go, despite planning life through words of affection and comfort to others, and by healing the wounded soul magically. That's why we find our differences interesting, but not necessarily true, as I'm sharing a little bit of what I'm feeling. Then again, I'm not so sure what exactly is the purpose, but I'm still going to embrace it as a positive outcome. The differences among ourselves are what connect us, because as humans, we all carry a curious side to our nature, and therefore become attractive to the what we believe: to be opposites without any measurements, per se.

Our intuition, our perception, our subconscious, and the outer world are the things that remain bigger and more mysterious than the limit of our comprehension. Bear with me on this: isn't this unknown "phenomena" what intrigues us more, for men have lived for millennium now. Yet it is because of our short span of life, our futile worries about the unnecessary, and our prejudicial pursuits that we progress only superficially "solo," instead of adjusting what's more important to us as a race of people. Blame our nature. Our self-awareness couldn't do it, so whom are we going to team up with? No matter what, it's purifying yourself to put in more, as we say, to build up more confidence and be prudent, competent, efficient, and perhaps charismatic. It's in our metabolism. Something has to give other than contradiction, insecurity, and confusion. We are not very sure about anything in concrete—we just speculate. Man lives day by day, making his own rules and stories to pass it onto others who gladly accept them, without questioning. It's bizarre.

With endless ideas of how to pursue a happy life, being more than just happy is having more meaningful and lasting answers that would better satisfy one's soul and mind, leading to self-completion in search of perfection. Again, as men, we act upon our reflection.

Let me be free and lead my way. Maybe some will follow; perhaps all should. My mission I was born with is still mine. Show me another way that is new, and I'll believe you. That's how we evolve: through manifestation in what we know and see, through our perception, intuition, faith, and belief, but mostly through things only you know. That unique you play a big part in this "theater" that is life. You also live it, because nobody else could, even if you wanted them to. This is yours, and yours only, so don't be scared to demonstrate it. Don't let your opportunity pass by; reason a way.

The Mysteries of Languages

There's an estimated six thousand or more languages spoken in the world today, not including local dialects. Mandarin Chinese is the most spoken language, followed by English, Spanish, Hindi, and Bengali.

Throughout history, whether through colonization, trade between countries, and any encounters between two different groups of people with a different culture and language, man has felt the need to connect the communication between them. To faster understand each other, they took shortcuts or simplified, form of language, meaning they took away most of the proper grammar and reduced words to areas of common interest. That's how pidgins were born: a much reduced language in attempt to avoid complications and bring different worlds of communication together.

Some languages were reduced to the point that they risked disappearing.

On the other hand, when pidgin becomes the main language of a population, new words are added, and new kinds of grammar reappear, and thus it becomes a Creole.

The difference between Creoles and pidgins is the fact that Creoles do not constitute solely the language of community, but they also express a cultural group in general. In different regions inside a country, local varieties of the national language may be used, which are called dialects. In some cases, it is not easy for linguists to distinguish between a language and a dialect.

Lingua francas are other ways to fill the gap among people communicating differently. Lingua franca is a common language used by groups whose mother tongues are different. These languages are inserted in diverse contexts within a community.

Some pidgins and creoles might and might not be considered lingua francas, depending how connected they are with the mother tongue, and therefore they might be considered official linguas francas.

Another linguistic factor is the result of many languages and dialect today, for example, many believe that Spanish is a modified version of Latin.

Communication is complex. Today, however, they are trying breaking down linguistic walls with a universal language, used often in international affairs between countries.

English and French are used more often in this scenarios We know that the whole world speaking one language is impossible for many reasons. On the other hand, linguistic walls might contribute to tension, discrimination, prejudice, or even war. However, languages show clearly that no man is superior to others, for they are all gifted with this divinely given skill. In its best moment, it's fascinating.

Today worldwide, an emerging number of people are learning new language for many reasons; some personal, some financial, some religious, and some just for fun. And some are "born" bilingual.

Sometimes learning a new language means you have to adapt and be open-minded, because it's deeply rooted in a new culture as well, and when done so, it also helps you see things from a new perspective—not necessarily right or wrong, but just different. Speaking a foreign language will help you reach out and make friends with people who speak the language and enjoy their companionship. How each one of us learns a new language varies, and for some it might be challenging, but believe that all the efforts are worth your while in many ways.

As mentioned before, it helps you view things from other perspectives, and it broaden your outlook about the world and life itself. Studies have shown that when learning a new language, your brain stays active, and it's a great exercise for keep young and active throughout life.

In particular, you can benefit from a new language, financially speaking, for there are many careers available, from teachers to translators, in diverse fields. This can bring the pleasure interacting with other people from different backgrounds, understanding their culture, adapting to it, and sharing all the possibilities that come with a new language "package" and endeavors. You feel a sense of belonging rather than an outsider.

Another area that greatly benefits from a foreign language is travel to a foreign country. While travel itself might not be a problem, rather it is the "getting around," such as ordering your own food, getting assistance from the public, emergencies, or simply asking someone out. You might encounter numerous of limitations if you're unfortunate enough not to learn new languages.

With today's world's demands, and with many people from many different cultures and language sharing same towns and cities, we shouldn't be limited to just a group of people because the lack of the language factor. The advantages are many, from personal fulfillment to business, travel, and financial success. And remember, it is a great way of staying forever young and active. What better reason than stay mentally in shape!

Language and communication are skills that need to be developed. Just like any other skills, some people tend easily to master a new language, and let's assume for some people it might be quite challenging.

In any case, it might take a long period to achieve fluency and proficiency, but it will be worth your while. The ability to communicate well is the backbone of any good relationship.

Academically speaking, any age would be a good age to learn a foreign language, or any new subject for that matter, but if we are referring to which age a person is better and faster at mastering a second language, then I would say as soon as you learn how to talk, per se, Because children adapt easily to new endeavors, and that includes learning a foreign language.

Children learn quickly. Rapid brain development occurs in children younger than three years of age. Everyday activities in a child's life, such as reading, singing, and playing, contribute greatly to a child's development and well being.

Studies indicate that the way a brain handles language, information, and emotions is *deeply linked with early childhood, and that's in part to great numbers of synapses generated at this stage of life. The more the brain is stimulated, the more there are connections.*

The brain also grows in size structure and function during these first few years. If a child is exposed to stimulating environment, "synaptic connections multiply, creating a broad network of neural pathways in the brain."

Reading aloud is also extremely good for language development in children, and since during the first years, young children develop mental attitudes that will influence their actions in the years to come, it is a parents' "job" to cultivate these good qualities and activities with their child, providing them with good, healthy mental nourishment.

The Brain expands enormously during these years, so does the area responsible for language, called the Wernicke's area and the Broca's area.

During the first years of life, the brain is like the big bang theory. It expands rapidly, absorbing everything it comes in contact with, that's why we should feed these young brains with good, solid material beneficial for a healthy development . In today's society, young children are being exposed to so much "garbage" from television, fancy toys, environment, and from many other sources.

As we know, language is fundamental to furthering a good relationship. It is the key that will open up new doors of success in our lives, and the best time to acquire these skills is during the very first years of a baby's life, and it is the parents' role to lay such foundation's, but unfortunately many parents neglect this crucial mental nourishment, thus probing development in areas such language.

Neurological circuits need stimulation to properly function, and when an individual is deprived of such regalia, a person will have a low and poor language-development skills, thus a more sedated life. So as you see, you need to engage your young child with plenty of healthy brain stimulation. Communicate well, and they'll take it from there to levels anew, because good language development means a good brain development in general.

Also in the early childhood, the brain generates great numbers of synapses, therefore making us capable of assimilating language, information, and emotions naturally. The more the brain is stimulated, the more are the connections. The brain also broadens in structure and function during these first few years, especially if a child is exposed to stimulating environment. "Synaptic connections multiply, creating a broad network of neural pathways in the brain."

Despite pronunciation, some researches shows that adults in some cases can learn a new language more efficiently than a younger learner, due to the danger of double semi-lingualism for early learners of a second language, who in some cases never had fully developed proficiency in both languages. When a new language is properly taught to young people, they can be both efficient and speak with a native-like pronunciation, which rarely happens with adults.

Even if you are fully grown up, it is possible to learn to convey your thoughts in a pleasant manner and to communicate effectively in a second language.

If you really desire to learn a new language, it is not only possible, but it can be a very stimulating and a very rewarding experience.

Hypothetically speaking, any age would benefit from acquire the skills of speaking a foreign language for many other reasons; whether the objective is personal fulfillment, business, travel, pursuing financial success, or just for fun, and it is also a great way of staying forever young and active.

Taking everything into consideration—the early age's adaptability, the dangers of double semi-lingualism for early learners of a second language, and adults' difficulties in pronunciation—it's been said that, overall, pre-adolescence, eleven to thirteen, would be the most favorable ages to learn a second language. Again, many factors are involved in each person, thus everyone's developments vary in learning a second language to a certain degree.

Imagine

If I could, anything. One thing.
What if I could eat from my mind?
It would be just glories and alleluias.
I wouldn't have to purchase pies for dessert,
Just benevolence in the morning.
A feast of loved food everyday.
A banquet full of exciting appetizers.
Instead of struggling for apples,
I would be reaching for stars.
Delighting with comfort and relaxation.

Instead of uncomfortable physical abnormalities, peace of
mind.
The light in my temple would always shine.
Rather than sickness and rumbling stomach, or guilty
conscious,
No worries for what I'm going to have tomorrow,
My mind would be full of good stocks.
Peace for breakfast, Happiness for lunch, repeat for dinner.
The odds.
With just the right amount of imagination,
and perhaps a good dose of love, tempered with fantasy
before dawn,
my plate full of contemplation, instead of contents.

Happy to share all I have with you.
No more veal for our meals.
For I'd rather fly off on my broom collecting space objects,
From there, spread them all over the starving children in
the world.
At this point, the earth full of aliments,
Occasionally I'll have a grape for variety.
Balancing opposite worlds, amused with laughter,
Instead of hungry eyes. It's your lucky day, for I've brought
you,
your favorite star, (SN 1995K).
Just another day with the greatest menu. Enjoy it
promptly.

If the universe could speak with me,
He would sough his problems to me.
He would tell me that sometimes he gets sick,
And don't know what's causing it, but it's
probably one's of the earthmen shenanigans.
He would tell me that the earth is his heart,
And God his brain that coordinates all its movements.
That his heart is a bit sick.
And without it, the brain can be vain and his own body to
waste.
Reason why, through sun, he provides good energy,
and oxygen for flowing,
And clean blood circulation throughout water cycles.

That some have been polluting, causing damage to his heart.

That was God to put earth under surgery before a chaotic earth attack,

And make it a new heaven.

He would also tell us that sometimes he's stressed and with a headache,

And he tries to relieve it causing a natural disaster.

But when he's happy, sunshine.

The universe is a body with a brain, and it's alive.

One question remains...

Could it be that the universe is conscious,

Changing accordingly with his bodily functions?

Reason why it's impossible for scientists/doctors to unravel all his mysteries.

The universe needs us,

So let's take care of ourselves,

Therefore our universe.

In the awakening,

One day, I'm going to wake up,

I had this strange dream,

That we were humans.

We lived with a heart, and we had all sorts of feelings.

And there was love amongst creatures.

They cared for each other,

And hated one another.

They lacked imagination.
They had dreams that they were dreaming.
It was really the Gaza daze.
They had many things,
A big soap opera,
We had all this kind of emotional attachments,
And we had worries.
And we used to compete against each other,
It was a true "rat race"
People had careers
And things.
Somehow they managed to educate themselves,
Like a group of sheep,
In a robotic way,
For they all most did the exact same thing or did nothing.
They set rules for themselves,
And force themselves to ways of society they created.
But they couldn't get out of the comfort zone,
And they did it for as many years,
Almost infinite time they followed,
They loved,
They worried,
And laughed,
They fought against each other.
They even set a limited time for themselves,
Where they "supposedly" perished from being,
They called it death.

They buried themselves in their deep subconscious,
To the point, they lost touch with their self-conscious "reality,"
Even six feet underground they remained unconscious.
But nobody knew,
That a living being will never go into extinction
For they will live in other's forms.
Everything they set in their heart and did exactly,
No question asked.
But it was real:
They felt it.
That is why they were scared to know more,
They also lived for an infinite time.
Some buried themselves with the idea of not taking so much pain,
Yes, suffering became their last dilemma.
Some gave up,
Every day was real.

I know I'm going to wake up
From this mindless game;
Waiting for my call
For I'm ready
To rise up from my unconsciousness.
I'm ready to tell my dream.
Till the wakening you will continue to worry,
To love and to wonder,

Everyday through generations,
"Life" was just a dream,
Just a mindless game.

Prisoner of my body,
Striving for freedom,
Plotting my escape
Wanting to be bodily free.
Why do I carry you around?
Dizzily I find myself
Running in circles.
I'm trapped in this body.

Today I left my "body" home intact
My soul, my spirit, and my imagination are with you.
I pictured you
Running errands.
I saw you thinking about me
when you felt my presence—
My soul free from my "burdened" body
(Heavenly father forgive my innocence
If I speak calamity)

Physically pure is vulnerability
And bestiality to the soul.
But the two are sensuality.
Let me take you to the midnight moon

In the summer solstice of August,
When the moon is bigger,
The sun shine shinier;
Brighter stars
Unmasking hidden secrets
And unifying the vast universe.
After a summer of adventures,
I return to my body.

Infinity

In the beginning, there was nothing, but one thing.

In the beginning there was only dark—

Deep and infinite dark spaces.

In the beginning, there were only a few things.

Everywhere was dark. Couldn't really see anything.

Nothing was visible in the beginning. Nothing was there.

In the beginning there was only one visible thing.

Empty dark, infinite space was the only visible things in the beginning.

Dark was also the only color, yet you manage to see it by your unconscious eyes.

You only had visions about infinite dark and empty spaces.

Your vision had also been for a long, infinite time.

But you couldn't see how you had begun to begin to have vision.

Another indefinite time you had. Slowly your eyes became conscious.

Now you really wanted to see, but you couldn't,

Unless dark, empty, and infinite space; really nothing.

And so it began.

Your eyes now started to think, but you wished for more.

Opened as wide as you could—Still nothing, only dark.
Through your eyes, you started to create imagination,
Slowly developing into thoughts, also for an infinite time.
As they grew bigger, without realizing it, you started to think.

You become aware with a conscious mind. You worry!
You began to imagine seeing other than just deep, dark, and infinite empty space. Also you started to think how...
Frustrated in an indefinite time in the dark empty space, you gave your all, suddenly your mind flashed. From inside of your mind you see, for the first time, other colors than dark. A color of a sparkling light flashed inside. Up until now, that was your first miracle, for you never saw anything before and couldn't possible have imagined it. In an infinite time, more color was created by your mind, together with imagination, but your mind couldn't stop anymore. More activity was wished upon you.

One day, frustrated, you, involuntarily and after impossible inexistent realization, wanted to touch the light, but it went through you. Lesson learned, let's move on. But perhaps more mind work would favor the beginning of all your creation. You start to contemplate such a magnitude of just a few colors and lights for an indefinite period of time. Through your eyes you start to feel delight subconsciously, but like the mind was developed, your heart was also developed, for the longest time.

In the beginning, it was just slight delights forever, then

your heart became aware of its feelings. Now you have deep and delightful feelings. Observing your own creation for infinite time, your eyes, heart, and mind, in conjunction with imagination, vision, and feelings, work together, so you wished to see, to feel and to create more as you go imagining into materializing and inventing more.

You were the artist, making arts from nonexistence into existence of things yet to come, now you materialized them into objects that can be felt, touched and seen—big, heavy objects everywhere in space. There was no limit of things in the infinite space. Remember that first star you created? And the joy felt after? No wonder you made numerous, to say infinite, numbers of them to compare to that infinite time lost unconsciously on that dark, empty, deep, infinite space. Look now. You were painting the space. You even painted a beautiful sky and put all kind of adornments around it; stars big and small, together and separate, spelling your own name. All the creation you also spelled with stars, so they remained yours. Constellations, as they call it nowadays, and galaxies, but you did it as you wrote and painted through your delights. You created everything and you made it look as if it were one big project. You know all its hidden places and mysteries. The word says it all. you made a verse of all things into one refrain: UNI-VERSE.

My Pledge to the World

Everyone has his or her own dreams. Trying to manifesting them in reality can sometimes be very discouraging.

There are many pathways and obstacles in the course of our lives, and sometimes choosing the right path can conflict with things we like to do or have, also called our "self's" being. We often let our "self" lose, pursuing some sort of praise. Talents are abandoned, creativity doesn't create anything, imagination turns into mere fantasies. Forgotten experience, I would say, means we aren't so free after all, and are slaving ourselves to many things, such as remunerable addiction, social tension, and fashion. Be obsessive, you might encounter a problem or two.

With Shakespeare, we learned soft-spoken, dexterous words. Great speeches given from a few distinguished leaders, and in the entertainment business, an angry black man exposes his life from the depths of his lungs. You know how it goes.

The key is to understand messages from others' experience in order to teach and discipline. Then again, knowledge is formed differently in every one of us, and therefore with different results and through different approaches. The point is to tolerate each other to support ones fault against us, to forget and forgive.

Until then, problems keeping on growing bigger, and people becoming more self-centered, haughty, I might say. The solution is in each one of us. To learn how to build up in-group, rather single-success individuals, leaving behind a more solid ground to the generations yet to come. We live in a "me" time, and that being said, it's a modern thing.

It is sad, yet true; describable, but not so easy to pass on.

Happiness comes from within.

Mysteries remain. How did we get to this uncaring and selfish human side? Where did we go wrong? An unsubordinated life free of greed, full of natural affection, is something that is inside of us, I believe, and is the sources that cause the battle with our inner peace and self-realization.

In the end, I would say that investing in ourselves and loved ones can be unambiguously wise. In the end, knowing you've been right all along, as well as an appreciation for your demise is indeed needed.

Other times, people are just not willing to cope. People only want you to have their leftovers.

Let's not part without mentioning crime scenes. Undefined and endless wars, blood drained, poisoning good soil—people's lives aren't anywhere near being spared under any circumstance possible, like hunger, homelessness, "everything." You know the list.

Theories about how to pursue a happy life are abundant, but sometimes a happy life is not having many houses, cars, and material gains, so to speak. Sometimes it is in the smallest thing you can think of. For some reason, it becomes a big part of that "hole" we need to fill.

Crimes diversify into types, motifs and personal attitudes.

The news we digest every day often involves crime of some sort, heard or unheard. Crime disparity, now more than ever, is skyrocketing, and anyone sane wonders what makes a person behave in such a way. Our society today is very stressful one, making an individual burst out easily.

Some crimes often involve violence, anticipated by an outburst of negative emotions, such as anger, stress, and rage, which are often associated with violence. Violence by itself is rarely the result of a crime; rather it's linked with personal attitudes and the accumulation of stress and other hidden reasons. Others become criminal because of greed, financial situations, or poor judgment.

The history of crime in an individual criminal might have long, past connections, or it might develop quickly if you let circumstance nourish it towards such behavior. When things don't go the way some might have expected, they might, misguidedly, turn to crime for answers.

If a person is unable to suppress what they feel or pass

over stress, it might result in some kind of emotional eruption, therefore causing "damages" crime wise. In today's society, crimes are portrayed in the media and neighborly to the extent that the values of individuals within that society will develop accordingly.

Studies have shown that "what we put in our mouths may also be nourishing anger. Cigarette smoking, alcohol consumption, and an unhealthful diet increase hostility. These epidemic lifestyle habits fuel stress and frustration, which erupts in the form of swearing, impatience, and intolerance. There are many unreasonable reasons that motivate a person to indulge in criminals behaviors, from misunderstandings, attitudes, vengeance, jealousy, rage, hate, personal "eeriness," chronic stress, or just having bad or unhealthy thoughts and consummating them, being poor or rich, or being black or white; none of this should be an excuse for a criminal mind. Crimes are unjustified, but criminals are to be justified. Unfortunately many criminals remain unidentified.

Some believe that human nature is inclined to do bad, and believe that it's in our genes and metabolism to be so, but I think is that it is what we let in our mind that greatly influences the decisions we make. It's the same reason I think it's wise to cultivate good and positives thoughts, no matter the situation, and to always remember: we shall overcome our frustration using better methods than indulging in crimes.

R.I.P

You lived heroic among us with a great attitude,
Oh, yes, you did,
But now that you are gone,
You remain unforgettable in our memories and hearts
perpetually.
We won't let you go. We can't.
We reminisce in all the goodies we shared.
Still we carry you in our hearts.
Troubled times. Happily, you left us an example.
No disguise will be needed.
We hold strong,
For now, time has changed.
Without you, it's not the same.
From a long-distance relationship
We hold you tight to our heart,
Separated by heavens and earth.
From angels flapping their wings,
To us clapping our hands,
We glorify you.
Such ambiguity.
Such closeness.
Can you hear our wrath?
Why? we ask in vain.
Tormented.

Rest in peace, my admirable.

Relentless shyness, yet magnificent.
Like mirror left on the sun, you shined,
How you dealt alone in life with your struggles.
Silently and bravely you let us out,
Because you cared so much,
True friend, only one, and forever shall it remain.
You are the North Pole, the brightest star in the sky
Safely guide my steps, don't let me trip, even in the dark.
Brilliant and radiant, such cleverness—
You can only be gifted.
Simplicity was your motto
Delicately you were chosen.
Easy knowing you, always open
Beyond measurement, yet so reliable to us.
The reason was what made you thick.
Innocent, childlike you approached life.
I still can't believe you are gone,
Without saying goodbye.
Your domain has parted to other dimension
Incompressible and unreasonable.
You are to be missed, my friend.

Death I wished upon myself
As you were gone, and left me alone in this world.
I can't forgive myself. Life has drawn the line.

The last card has been played.

My world is coming to an end.

The results are in; there is no need to "pack" my bags.

Please look down to me, as I bow down, looking up for you,

Watch my pain; tell me you are better now.

Let your request be my life's path, and then I can relieve my cargo.

Defeated by our last enemy,

Unmercifully, a knife through my heart.

My friend, I'll be missing you indeterminately.

I couldn't give you better than what was in store for you,

Waiting behind heaven's gates,

You were my angel at first.

Now I know we can both smile and rejoice

until we meet up again very soon.

Justice will be fair.

Earth will be a new heaven.

Our friendship is an eternity.

Bless you, my comrade, peacefully you rest with me.

Live By the Moment

"Yesterday is the past, and tomorrow is the future.

Today is a gift—that's why they call it the present."

Do not be anxious about tomorrow, said Jesus Christ, for tomorrow will look after itself. Of course that doesn't mean we shouldn't think about tomorrow, but it clearly stated the importance of not being anxious or too worried about what tomorrow holds.

"Stop being anxious about your souls as to what you will eat or what you will drink, or about your bodies as to what you will wear...Observe intently the birds of heaven, because they do not sow seed or reap or gather into storehouses; still your heavenly Father feeds them..."

Who of you, by being anxious can add one cubit to his life span?

We stress about tomorrow, and we worry and plan about our future, but the concept of time's overrated. Tomorrow starts now. Don't even think about tonight, think about this instant moment now. Now is time, now is the only time you can be certain of, now go ahead and feel. Live it and love it, and quit all tomorrow's will.

Never be anxious about tomorrow, because anxiety will not help you resolve anything you're facing, but on the contrary will mostly worsen your situation. Sometimes when we feel anxious about tomorrow, we forget about the things we could do today.

Let tomorrow come, if it comes. Let it happen, for you do not know what tomorrow will give birth to. We need to be practical, because many things we worry about never happen—just futile worries. The truth is, it's much wiser to live each day as it comes, especially when the pressures and problems we face could create anxiety in us.

We all are aware of our necessities in life, and we all somehow try to pursue them, but how many plans have we made that never had a slightest chance coming to fruition?

There are things we won't yet live to see; dreams shattered, accidents, natural disasters, diseases, and more; my point being that we don't know what tomorrow will bring, or if it will be another tomorrow. Sometimes waiting for tomorrow can be a waste of time and life itself.

Imagine you were given only one day to live, and you want to live it to the fullest, with no worries and no attachments for tomorrow. At the end of that day you would be glad you had good time. Sometimes that's what life really is, one big day with breaks for sleep and such, but the same day progress, and tomorrow never exists.

But with life comes responsibilities. We have to feed and shelter ourselves and clothe our kids, and I'd be a liar if I told you I don't have big dreams and big plans. But for today there's no stressing about that, for the day's almost through, and I'm just not going to worry about it.

Tomorrow? Maybe, but I still doubt it. For now, why not pour another glass of wine, turn on the music on a low beat, and enjoy this moment like there's no tomorrow.

This moment is your life. Life is this moment, and this moment only. Live by this moment and for it. Dedicate your all to it. Be thankful for this moment and this moment only. Think about it. Feel the heartbeat, look around you, and think about how many moments have passed, and now you only have this moment left. I know if I could, I would "hug" this moment.

Drink your wine, feel its outcome in your brain and in everything you visualize. But no matter how disturbed you might be, try and feel this moment. Live it, feel it, love every single breath, for each one of them worth a life, which is one breath. Each breath is one moment; each moment is life, and it's all happening now. You can't reverse time nor forward it. Time is fixed; time is you in this moment.

You don't know any other time for sure. Take a deep one. I couldn't have asked for more or better, because I'd probably forgotten one of the ingredients of life, so when I combined all my energy add my wisdom—when I put my mind together with my brain, it's beyond existential. It's funny when everything is there within you, but so hard to find sometimes. It's all in there. Dig deep. Try to find the true meaning of yourself, your destiny and your role that was set from the beginning in your heart that you maybe haven't developed yet, haven't played it right, because you were too worried about what others think. Know that they, too, misjudge themselves, and they want you to be the way they are. That was not your purpose in this life, so stop thinking of others if they can't cope.

You don't have to fight on the same level because some birds. Just fly higher than others, and even if they want to pick on you, they can't reach you. You don't want go down to their level to fight with them. You just keep on flying higher and higher, and you simply win, because your enemies can't fly as high as you. But this not about winning over your enemies. This is about joy of life. Live to the fullest, which can only mean that every breath counts. Every one of them is fulfilling, and you're grateful to be a part of this cause.

You can't imagine that billions didn't even have a chance to become part of existence, so we are lucky. Sometimes I don't even know what I'm complaining about. Sometimes it's over things I don't really need, and if I do, it wouldn't really matter. In this logic, it's impossible to catch up with time, because the moment is not the actual time. It's all about the moment. You've known that moment is gone, and it will never come back, and this one is gone now, too. Now is now. Now is the moment we live in, only now. Now is gone. Hopefully another now comes, and we'll be able to catch it.

Homelessness

Lying on the city sidewalk,
The thick grass matched my beard,
Resembling
No sign of a riverside,
Except the human traffic
Thumping loudly, gigantic,
My ear glued to the floor
Inculpable of homeliness
My cola can filled with whiskey,
Freed me from thy pain.
Couldn't be happier.
So was the world
Misled from my "grief"
And my watery eyes
from the local paper cigarettes,
Wishing one day
to dance on my grave.
My plan was to be different
A nonconformist with the world's demands
Wish to be "free as a bird"
Breaking society's chains
as I humbly struggle the hues of shrewdness
In which consists my world.
For the rest,

I *continue to be*
"A *man without a plan.*"
From the lattice of my imagination
I *spotted calumniation*
As I *peered down*
As *for to*
I'm *rotting in the Sheol of earth*

There I sat,
Here I think,
Act I shall,
upon thy thoughts
before dost perish
and my seat moves.
"I think therefore I am"
Now here I am,
and there I was:
Golden me,
silver line,
whereas crowned my foot.
Steered pavement,
every step's a lifetime.
"Wherever you go, there you are."
Rested eyes
see invisibility.
A crossed world
Where you are

or not.
"To be or not to be."
Think I know
I will not be limited
by my own thoughts.
The best's still in me.
Return, I beg you,
to me.
Refuse to the chase.
My case will always be
I'm awaiting, beloved of myself.

The Way You Love Me

Beneath a torrid sun,

under the blue sky,

A scintillated ocean shushes its passerby.

Across a stunning lush valley,

Its mist currents draw up dreams to reality.

As I dive into the deep green,

I hear humming from the shell's house underneath.

Its waves with a bright smile,

Wobbling down, open arms,

Welcoming gathered people,

From its moister sand, in woos.
Limited by my own consciousness,
I can't extend it as far as I could remember.
The first time we saw
Just a glimpse, were you
Yet distinctive?
I didn't conceive you,

Nor deceived you,

Perhaps innocently I granted you,

My blurry mind couldn't discern "the" clearly you.

Like in a crowded street,

so many

come and go.

From time to time,

Disappear as quickly as formed,
Re-birthing oneself.
It's a mystery you hung there.
You have faith in yourself
And, I must say, empowered my faithfulness.
Contagious,
Filled me hope
That we'll make it someday.
Unconditionally you loved me,
Like I love you.

Now there's a kiss awaiting on mountain's atop.
If you believe in the midnight moon,
Next day's anew.
The after-rain
Caught us
Sitting on a rainbow.

Touching the silk soft sky
The way your skin-tone flows
Makes me glow
I can't believe ,
I finally have to say
The old saying:
It might be love
Then what is?

It got me feeling the blues
And thinking the hues
From Georgia to Cincinnati.
It got me singing
On my way to California.
Lady New York
Is on my mind.

The arc of love
On our feet,
Coming to the valley of humanity,
Where everything is real
But in heaven was made before:
A love union.
No men can divide.

I know,
I swear,
And I promise
I'll love you
forever
And ever,
No matter,

Deprived, I keep on trying.
Derived, I strive to thrive in life.
That's the line I choose to define: such a fine sunshine

under the sunlight.

When you arrive, I smile.

Because you are mine, till I die, and I'll never let you cry.

Neither I would lie; I'm not that type. Baby, you're my life, I promise to be kind,

Cause you are so fine to the spine.

I let go of my pride and become your sweet pie.

Politely, I'll call you cutie-pie,

And together we'll rise and shine.

You and I,

We decided to make tonight,

And the rest of our life,

Our best nights.

Sipping that fine wine after a bite,

Listening to "I just Died in your arms tonight."

Outside, near the fire, and from inside candlelight.

Looking high up in the sky as a dive into divine.

I see a light as my guide.

I will hold you in my heart tight.

Let's not let this moment die,

Through another sunrise,

So let's ride. It's all right.

Staring at your eyes

And I can't deny

Neither am I shy to testify

This vibe as my plight.

Life would be unworthy otherwise,
And the pain would be dire.
I do not want to say goodbye,
It is not satisfying,
Cause we have such a short time.
So bright and wise, this feels so right.
You are my type, and I'll be kind.
If loving you was a crime,
I wouldn't mind to do the time.
This is my life I write black in white,
Making lines rhyme on the mike.
Have to survive, with you by my side,
We can make it to the other side of life.
We cannot be divided.
You and I are alike,
And we'll be together for eternal life.

"Together We Stand" (A document)

I took the liberty of writing this "document." This should be a document that should be preserved for the rest of our lives, through generations. And like our forefathers' declaration of independence and humans rights are all preserved as sacred to us, this will be called "the intervention," or "the holiday," and before leaning towards its details, I'll leave you with some well-known observations.

From the beginning of time, the human race has always been split apart, among and from itself. And as we live on, we become more and more divided into a lot of sub-mini-groups of all sorts, from our beliefs, practices, misconceptions and differences; the quotidian making of choice, the desirable things, and the things we are fond of. We are separated into fields of religion, medicine, other beliefs, and in every subject under the sun. It seems always to be a contradiction; one will disagree with another and take different path based on self-beliefs, and others will follow. Another group has formed, the other loses a member or two, and so on.

There's never been a single time on earth that everybody agreed on one subject of matter, or have participated in an event of any given chance that as a whole race. Instead, sub-mini-groups thus separate us, and somehow I believe that weakens our powers and therefore our achievements and accomplishments as a race together, rather than as self-individual ("me time").

"Together we stand."

I also believe that as a race, we have some powers, but those same powers have been split apart among us, leaving us powerless.

Can a single individual accomplish great things in life through his beliefs and willpower? I'm in position to make assumptions that, if we put our strength and beliefs together as a whole race, we can overcome and achieve greatness.

The devil is a powerful creature, but he doesn't work alone, but in togetherness. He does all his work with his demons and angels. We all know God himself works with spiritual creatures and angels to do more, so we too should work together in order to transcend. That's where my mind is triggering, and I might just have found a way to do so. We are going to have to agree in one subject, I mean everybody has to come together on this to make it happen.

For some people have a clear understanding about the human race's origin and its purpose and meaning of life in general. We all are familiar with questions related: where did we come from, why, and where do we go? For most people, life is far more mysterious than it looks, and they demand and seek answers during their lifetime in many ways. our natural curiosity is not just an accident. Somehow all humans believe in other dimensions of life. I can positively say we all believe in something. You don't have to be religious nor indifferent to believe; you believe anyway. We all do, even non-believers, whether we are Buddhist, Catholics, Jewish, Muslims, Mormons, Protestant, skeptics, or just "spiritual" people.

Doctors are divided by mini-fields to classify themselves, their social services, and their status—an eye doctor is nothing like an ear doctor, and so on. We are divided into thousands and thousands of pieces. Some groups are so small they are barely groups, just names and domains. My point being that we all believe in something. The right from wrong is the main issue.

What are we going to do to better our lives and the lives of our fellow men?

I say we need to have an intervention with our spirits. We need to call our what we call "superiors." We need to demand from our guides our angels, that it's time to have a meeting with our gods. This is not just a theory but to make a reality. Let's set up a date and time for this intervention, for this meeting

With that in mind, we are going to use all of our strength, our faith, and our powers to call upon the unknown world, the other dimension, and our spirits. Whatever your belief is, it's time to come together as a whole human race, so in this day, at the same time, same minute, and same second, all humans should take a few seconds of their life and try this practice.

I say everybody, whether you are Catholic or Protestant, Muslim or other. We are going to pray, and most relevant, we are going to demand answers for our race from the unknown world. Whatever it's your question or worry, this day it should come forward, because you are going to remember that almost seven billion others are in this with you, at the same time, same day, at this very moment, with the same objective. And I'm sure the world will be different the very next morning. Pray for the poor, for the suffering, and injustice, and for everything else that deprives you in any way. Don't just pray for yourself. Pray for our race, pray for a better world, pray or do your ceremony—or should I say demand better, because we deserve it. And its not our fault we live in a world that we live in. Our guidance and deliberation has left us here to deal alone in this vast universe, so now the time has come to call upon them. Wherever ceremony you do and believe works for you, let's do it on this day at this same time. I'm not saying to change your religion, your beliefs. All I'm saying is let's execute them all at the same time, knowing the day of intervention, the day we came along. This day should also be celebrated every year. We have tried everything, but more personal than in groups, and there is nothing better than one big group: the humankind, our kind. We, too, have powers. Remember: "together we stand."

What do you say? Are you with me on this? If yes, let's spread the word and make it official. We also need a specific time so we all can join in together, on this day, at this same time. And perhaps we more details, and rewriting this documentation may be necessary, for I am here hereby, and let's watch tomorrow happen.

"Do not become unevenly yoked with unbelievers…

What harmony is there between Christ and Belial?

Or what portion does a faithful person have with an unbeliever?" Said Paul: "Make sure of all things; hold fast to what is fine." (2 Corinthians 6:14, 15; 1 Thessalonians 5:21)

Perhaps the idea of joining a religion is the question— whether certain ways of worshiping matter. If you sympathize with the way God is worshiped by a determinate religion in particular and their different wavelengths in comparison, then the question whether to join or not to join?

Ideas and beliefs diverge, like whether you should or shouldn't join a religion in order to believe or to serve God. Questions arise: do we need to or have to be a member of certain organization to serve the purpose of a God? Some think and confirm that you don't have to associate with one particular religion to believe, and they claim that sometimes they get closer in touch with God through meditation, nature's way, or others, rather than in participating in a religious ceremony in a church. Others believe sincerely that you have to be a part of a religion to serve god, and also think that is not just an academic matter, but a vital one. But more questions arise: if there is a need to join, which religion should you join? Is there only one true religion? How do you identify it?

Since all this revolves around God, wouldn't it be wiser if we try to know what the author, god, says about all this through his word—in this case the bible?

Lots of people think that all religion have the same purpose, and that's to take you to God, since most of them believe that there's only one God, and therefore the choice of an organization, even though important, doesn't make a difference.

That might have a bit of logic when we realize that there's only one God, but we have to remember that many religions have different points of view, different teachings, and even sometimes are very contradictory with another. It's almost that they believe in different things and have different practices and requirements.

These differences can be so big that they find it hard to believe what other groups teach, to the point of ignoring each other.

In biblical times. Differences also emerged between religious groups. In Corinthians, Paul admonished, "I exhort you, brothers, through the name of our Lord Jesus

Christ that you should all speak in agreement, and that there should not be divisions among you, but that you may be fitly united in the same mind and in the same line of thought."

On that prerogative and many other examples followed by Jesus and his disciples, I think it is important and beneficial to choose the right religion, and that can't be achieved by disagreements and coercive manners that we see in diverse religions.

We have to identify which religion brings people of kinds together, regardless of their culture, race, and origin. We need to ask ourselves what religion isn't involved in wars (killing), or have sided with some political views. Jesus said, "My kingdom is not like this world affair."

I do believe there is one true religion, we all will have a chance to participate, and in delivering God's news, it will be brought to each one of us so that we have a chance to join. But it doesn't necessarily mean we have to join to attain God's approval, and be saved.

The world as a decoy

The world as a decoy,
From the beginning to the end;
From the cut of umbilical cord,
To six feet under.
Human race, doomed, released into this world,
Our best resort
It's our faith, to better it.
Taken as a lasting treasure.
When things couldn't get worse,
We still hoped for a better day.
Holocaust we created for ourselves
As we head, thrilled for self-destruction
From corruption to war, crimes and poverty
Around our neck,
Makes me wonder what's next,
Perhaps the Armageddon?
'Till then, we will continue to die.
We will continue to kill each other.
We will continue to live in poverty,
Disease, and war.
Innocent lives will be in no way spared.
Millions of children will starve some more.
But hope we must,
And live we try,

Perhaps they'll have mercy on us and spare us,

But no promises are on the horizon,

And no need to pretend:

Just cruel reality

Making innocents shed undeserving tears

In this atomic era—

Era of treats and attempts;

An era of uncertainties and fear

Who is to be plotted next?

In the next second, whose daughter/son is going to be starving to death?

In the next month, who we will battle against?

New regime in a few years,

Just as a facet from being called dictatorial

New lies, new promises, some even new hopes, at least no surprise,

For we have taken so much,

And we can only take so much.

Our strengths are wearing off with centuries of multilane,

So next time you see your commander on that podium,

Ask him to yourself,

"Who are you fighting for?"

In this critical time

Modern time has become

Indeed hard times to deal with.

We dwell on

Protecting our fort. We must

Not with weapon of destruction,
But with hope we surrender ourselves,
Choosing our battles carefully,
For life's not a game of poker—
We hold on our chips
Nonetheless shan't fold
Where "the pen becomes mightier than the sword,"
Avoiding being dissipated
And crying in dissolution
The failures we anticipated
Against our worthy adversary,
We keep pushing
'till the gate of impasse passes
Through our fingertips,
And the footprints abandon
To anew era
Peace of mind
And peace for all and goods.

Redemption

Our delights and dislikes are unlike.
The reason why confusions arise,
But I bare with you through our fights,
So we prosper to survive.
The currents of life instead of the currency of spites.
You despise my likes,
I criticize your hypes,
But at the end, we can say we survived,
Side by side,
Parallel lines,
Separate lives.
No need to take my life with your knife.
In peace you go with your life,
Friend-of-mine.

My eyes have seen too much.
My mouth has shared enough.
My actions overpower me.
My life is on the line
My manners do not matter.
My words are just words,
Like everything is nothing
Is when I put my passion in action.
The effect ends nowhere.

My ambitions, my pride, are in a deep fight with my soul,
Just to crush me even more. Deserting me,
Reducing to dust.
In this battle, I am defeated
Until I find the line that separates thy confusion.
In the beginning, the idea was for a happy life. I asked,
What made it painful?
Endless ideas in how to pursue a happy life
Try to find that missing puzzle,
For it remains a mystery.
Go with the flow,
I said politely, it could be fascinated,
As I wave away with a smile in my eyes.

Redeem first thyself to reign the unachievable,
Out of misery towards enlightenment,
A handful of bluster aroused,
Inciting unprovoked confusion.
Feelings starting to chipper,
Becoming distraught,
Gone and forgot what exactly...
Struggling and hustling might be "healthy,"
But forging and scrounging is venom;
Let me drink thy poison
That succumbed my insides,
'Till I'm vexed from sobriety,
That makes me deluded.

Why the angst?

Who's calumniating against thee?

My portfolio yet to be completed...

In the midst of all,

I find serenity,

"Because True happiness isn't to be shaken nor stirred."

I stand tall in the middle of all insanity,

I remain strong till whenever,

For I'm to know awareness,

From everything, even the unknowns.

Know when, where, and how,

But perhaps mostly know that

We are who we are.